Punxsutawney Phil and Malcomb Bud Dunkel,
President, Punxsutawney Groundhog Club

This book has been written and published, and this photograph and footprint reprinted, with the permission of the Inner Circle of the Punxsutawney Groundhog Club of Punxsutawney, Pennsylvania—"The Original Weather Capital of the World (since 1887)."

This book
belongs to:

_____

THE STORY OF

PUNXSUTAWNEY PHIL

"THE FEARLESS FORECASTER"

by
Julia Spencer Moutran, Ph.D.

illustrated by
Marsha Lewis Dubnansky

Copyright © 1987 by Julia Spencer Moutran, Ph.D. Reprinted, 1988; 1989; 1990; 1991; 1994
All rights reserved.
PRINTED IN THE UNITED STATES OF AMERICA.

Library of Congress Cataloging
in Publication Data
Library of Congress Catalog Number: 86-82950

Moutran, Dr. Julia Spencer
Groundhogs, Groundhog Day, Hibernation, Woodchucks
SUMMARY: Family of three groundhogs works together to prepare winter burrow, hibernates as
a family, and world famous Punxsutawney Phil awakens on Groundhog Day to dramatically
predict if spring has come.
1. Science—Juvenile Literature.
(1. Groundhogs. 2. Groundhog Day. 3. Hibernation. 4. Woodchucks.) I. Title.
First Book in the Series: THE STORY OF PUNXSUTAWNEY PHIL.
ISBN 0-9617819-0-4, paperback   ISBN 0-9617819-2-0, hardback
ISBN 0-9617819-3-9, audiocassette Coronet Film (16mm) and Video, #6594C
Series Number: 0-9617819-1-2
Second Book in Series: WILL SPRING EVER COME TO GOBBLER'S KNOB?
ISBN 0-9617819-4-7, paperback   ISBN 0-9617819-5-5, hardback
ISBN 0-9617819-6-3, audiocassette

Illustrated by Marsha (Dubansky) Sweetland

Additional copies may be purchased by calling Literary Publication 1-800-203-READ, or using the Order
Form in the back of the book.

To Punxsutawney Phil,

on his 100th birthday . . .

and to Meredith,

on her 5th.

CHAPTER ONE

Meet Punxsutawney Phil,
The Famous Groundhog

Punxsutawney Phil scampered across the open field next to Mr. Beiler's vegetable garden. His grizzly brown fur was warmed by the autumn sun.

He sat up and noticed the alfalfa and soybeans that were still growing. He looked toward the mountains and the skyline, noticing the new colors in the leaves.

Everything in Punxsutawney, Pennsylvania had a golden autumn glow.

Phil saw his neighbor, Seymour Squirrel, planting acorns. He too sensed the changing season as he hurriedly hid acorn after acorn.

Phil rushed toward the edge of the woods. His stout body disappeared into a thicket in the woods.

There he saw his cousin Barney gnawing on some hay. He was using his chisel-like teeth to break the pieces into smaller ones.

"Getting ready for the frost?" asked Phil.

"I thought I'd make a new pillow this year," replied Barney.

"Where's Philomena?" asked Phil.

"I think she's still basking in the sun," said Barney, pointing to the edge of the woods.

Philomena was stretching in the sun. She liked to take a rest in the noon sun before looking for food in the afternoon.

"Phil!" squealed Philomena, eager to tell her husband the news:

"Wilbur Weasel was over at our winter burrow at Gobbler's Knob. I saw **his footprints** in the dirt around the rocks."

"If Wilma Weasel thinks her family is getting **our burrow** this year . . . ."

"Calm down, Philomena," assured Punxsutawney Phil, confident as always. "Tomorrow we'll go over to Gobbler's Knob and prepare the burrow. I sense *frost* is on the way."

Phil, Philomena and Barney had spent many winters at Gobbler's Knob. Phil was even born there on February 2, 1887. This was their special winter home and no one was going to take it away from them!

Bright and early the next day, Phil, Philomena and Barney went over to Gobbler's Knob.

Phil started examining the *secret* entrance to the burrow. Rocks and sticks disguised the opening, but Phil spotted Wilbur Weasel's footprints. He also noticed *others'*.

"Look, Phil," shouted Barney examining the new footprints. ***"Fox prints!"***

Philomena let out a piercing *whistle!*

"Relax, Philomena," assured Phil. "You are in no danger. Mr. Fox isn't here. He just passed by. I'll build a new tunnel and exit today, just in case we have any problems."

Phil pushed the soft dirt with his powerful feet. He started kicking dirt aside, opening the front burrow door. The opening to the home was barely visible.

Once the door was open, Phil helped Barney slide down the tunnel into the living room. Barney had a slight limp from injuring his leg over the summer.

Philomena squeezed herself into the opening.

"I think I need a little push, Dear," requested Philomena. She had been eating lots of green vegetation over the summer, and had put on a few extra pounds.

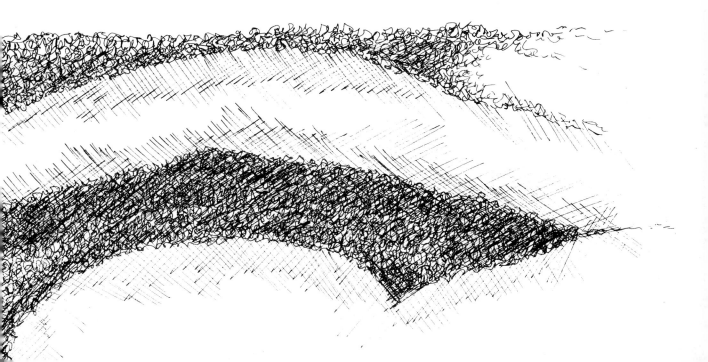

Once inside, each groundhog set to do his routine chores. Barney's job was to clean out the living room and bathrooms. Phil's job was to inspect the structure of the home and build or repair their tunnels and secret exits.

Philomena was in charge of storing a few items for the
kitchen, like clover and dandelions—just enough to tide
them over until they went into a *deep winter's sleep*.

It was Philomena's job to decorate the home as well!

"These leaves will never do," exclaimed Philomena in disgust.

"Look at these ugly brown leaves on the bed! All broken too!"

Phil was busy checking the angle of the tunnels. They had to lead upward at an incline so water did not seep into the burrow.

Phil worked for several hours digging a new "secret" exit. It was always a good idea to have more than one back door!

Philomena tapped Phil on the shoulder.

"I was just outside gathering some maple, birch, and scarlet oak tree leaves. What do you think of yellow for the living room, scarlet for our bedroom, and red for Barney's room?"

Phil loved to sleep on the leaves and hay that Philomena used to make their beds. Last year they had an orange bedroom. This year scarlet sounded great!

Before late afternoon, Phil, Philomena and Barney finished their chores. Phil carefully sealed the entrance door to the burrow.

They had worked hard to fix their home for the cold winter ahead. Now they would enjoy the last few days of autumn.

On the way home Phil sensed the coolness of the afternoon air. *A special chill could be felt.*

"Let's go over to Mr. Beiler's garden for dinner,"
suggested Barney, thinking about the celery that was still
growing.

Philomena and Barney followed Phil as he led the
way.

Only a few weeks remained before the groundhogs
would leave their summer home in the woods. Soon they
would spend the winter at Gobbler's Knob.

Then it would be Phil's special day—*his birthday!*
On this day in February, he would appear at the entrance
to his burrow. *Then* he would make his much awaited
forecast . . .

**Would spring be here? Or, would winter stay
longer?**

**Only Phil, the Fearless Forecaster, would
decide.** It was always up to him to let his neighbors and
the other animals know his prediction!

Everyone would await his forecast on Groundhog
Day. . . .

CHAPTER TWO

The Winter At Gobbler's Knob

One night in early October Punxsutawney Phil was restless. He couldn't sleep. He tossed and turned.

He got up and looked at the Harvest Moon. The moon lit the Pennsylvania farmlands.

Phil loved his home. He loved the fields and the woods.

He looked forward to next spring too. He had watched Mr. Beiler and his family with their harvesting and planting for spring. Next year there would be lots of edible vegetation.

Maybe Philomena and he would start their family in the spring!

The next night the air seemed colder. Phil awoke around midnight. He tiptoed over to Philomena and nudged her.

"*Tonight* is the night. We must leave ***now!***" whispered Phil.

In the still of the night, Phil led Philomena and Barney over to Gobbler's Knob. He looked up at the moon, knowing it would be a long time before he saw it again.

Phil kicked the dirt and moved the rocks away to expose the entrance way to their burrow. No footprints anywhere! They had done a good job concealing their home.

Down the three of them slid into the living room.

It was Phil's job to seal the entrance to the burrow. Reaching for the last bit of dirt with his front paws, he carefully sealed the front door shut!

No one knew that they had moved into their burrow during the night!

Here at Gobbler's Knob they would be comfortable. Here they would have the warmth and quiet they needed during the winter months.

For the next few nights they enjoyed the greens that Philomena had stored. But there weren't many of them to eat. And, the three of them were very full anyway.

Feeling sleepier and sleepier, Barney and Philomena
retired to their bedrooms and soon fell asleep. Phil could tell
they would not wake up until the spring.

Phil took one last inspection of the burrow and lay down to rest. He was satisfied with the improvements they had made to their burrow.

He smiled. Here he was again at Gobbler's Knob. It felt good to be home again!

Phil yawned and stretched. He was very content. He closed his eyes and fell into a deep sleep.

The days grew colder and colder. Winter had come to Gobbler's Knob. Snow fell to the ground, covering the farmlands and mountains.

Mr. Beiler's children sleighed and played near Gobbler's Knob. Beneath the ground, inside the burrow, Phil and his family slept quietly and peacefully.

Days and weeks passed. Then months. Soon it was the end of January. *Phil's birthday was coming soon!*

Suddenly, something moved in the burrow. The crunching of leaves could be heard!

Phil rolled over on his side. The leaves and hay beneath him were brittle. He opened his eyes slowly, focusing on the bedroom wall.

Phil reached and felt the earth. It felt softer and warmer. He knew what that meant!

"It must be near spring. I wonder if winter is over," he thought.

Phil stood up slowly. He looked down and noticed he had lost a lot of weight. He felt a pang of hunger.

Phil looked at Philomena. She was still in a deep winter's sleep. He listened and heard Barney snoring in the other bedroom.

Phil didn't want to wake his wife or cousin. It might be *too soon* for them to get up.

"Well, it looks as though I'm the *first* one awake, as usual," thought Phil.

"It can't hurt to take a little peek outside and see what's going on. I need some fresh air anyway."

Punxsutawney Phil climbed up the tunnel to the front door of the burrow. He scratched and he scratched at the sealed door, opening it slightly. The dirt moved slowly, but *predictably*.

And then, Punxsutawney Phil popped his furry head
right out of the hole!!

He looked quickly to the left. He looked quickly to the right. Sensing no danger, he climbed out of the burrow and stood on the snow-covered ground.

Phil rubbed his eyes and started moving forward. Then he stopped in his tracks.

As he stood up on his hind legs, the sun was shining behind him.

He glanced at the ground.

Something moved *very slowly* . . .

Something dark and eerie . . .

SOMETHING EVEN BIGGER THAN PUNXSUTAWNEY PHIL!!

His *shadow!* It was Phil's very own shadow darkening the snow-covered ground.

The cold wind blew and chapped Phil's nose. He looked for Mr. Beiler's farm: **no signs** of the horses and plows working the fields; **no signs** of the family in the garden.

Phil thought about his cozy, warm burrow under the ground. He thought about Philomena and Barney, curled and nestled in their beds.

Phil knew it was *too soon* to wake them. He knew winter was not over. Years of living at Gobbler's Knob told him this year was no different.

Better to return to his warm burrow underground.
Better to sleep awhile longer.

*Then spring would be on its way. Then it would be time
to wake the others.*

Phil turned and squinted as he faced the morning sun. The brightness seemed even brighter after months of darkness underground.

As Phil turned, his long shadow loomed behind him.

He walked toward the burrow opening and started his descent.

And, as Punxsutawney Phil disappeared into the burrow, *he took his shadow with him!*

The Fearless Forecaster had made his weather prediction . . .

SIX MORE WEEKS OF WINTER!

THE STORY OF PUNXSUTAWNEY PHIL TRIVIA CARDS
THE FOLLOWING TRIVIA CARDS CAN BE REPRODUCED ON BOTH SIDES AND CUT.

1.
Q. Can groundhogs swim and climb?

2.
Q. What is the average litter size of young groundhogs?

3.
Q. If a groundhog sees its shadow, what does that mean?

4.
Q. How much do groundhogs weigh (range of weight)?

5.
Q. What are two other common names for groundhogs?

6.
Q. Groundhogs belong to what scientific order and family?

7.
Q. How many upper and lower teeth (incisors) does a groundhog have?

8.
Q. What color are the groundhog's teeth?

9.
Q. How does a groundhog's burrowing help the soil?

10.
Q. What sounds does the groundhog make when it is alarmed?

11.
Q. How many coats of hair does the groundhog have?

12.
Q. When the baby groundhogs are born, can they see?

13.
Q. When a groundhog hibernates, its heartbeat drops from 80 beats per minute to how many?

14.
Q. What foods does a groundhog like to eat?

SUGGESTION: ONE TRIVIA QUESTION A DAY FOR 2 WEEKS PRIOR TO FEB. 2!

2.
A. 4 to 9—(Generally about 5)

1.
A. Yes

4.
A. 4 to 14 Pounds—(Heaviest in Autumn with Stored Fat)

3.
A. 6 More Weeks of Winter!

6.
A. Order: Rodentia
   Family: Sciuridae

5.
A. Woodchuck and Whistle-pig

8.
A. White

7.
A. 4 Incisors—2 Upper; 2 Lower

10.
A. It whistles.

9.
A. It aerates and turns the soil.

12.
A. Blind until about a month old.

11.
A. Two—Coarser on Top; Softer, Underneath.

14.
A. Alfalfa, Soybeans, Herbs, Grasses, Danelions, Clover.

13.
A. 4 to 5

THE HISTORY OF PUNXSUTAWNEY PHIL

As early as February 2, 1887, the first annual visit to Gobbler's Knob was made by believers in Punxsutawney Phil. Since that date, Phil's annual forecasts have been recorded in newspapers, broadcast on radio stations, and filmed for television stations across the world.

Below is a picture of Gobbler's Knob with Phil's name on the burrow door. Thousands of people gather in the early hours of the morning on February 2. Some arrive to stake their spots the night before. Everyone wants a prime view of the famous Phil, and the atmosphere is exciting as spectators await Phil's appearance.

The Home of Punxsutawney Phil, Gobbler's Knob, where Phil appears every February 2.

Fourteen members of the Inner Circle of the Punxsutawney Groundhog Club march in line and are escorted by the National Guard. They are dressed in top hats and formal tuxedos, their required attire as dignitaries greeting The Fearless Forecaster.

As they march and take their places around the entrance to the burrow, the spectators and believers in Phil know the moment for which they have been waiting has finally arrived. Cheers and calls for The Seer of Seers fill the air!

Punxsutawney Groundhog Club Inner Circle Members, Kneeling L to R: Bill Deeley, Phil's Handler; Bud Dunkel, Club President. Standing L to R: Bill Roberts, Bill Anderson, Bob Roberts, Mike Johnston, Paul Johnston, Bud Murray, Bob Chambers, Bill Cooper, Jack Dereume, Harry Philliber, Chris Lash, Keith Shields.

The President of the Inner Circle welcomes those present and gives a short introductory speech. Then the Handler of the Groundhog prepares to open the door to the burrow. The President knocks on Phil's door with a gnarled acacia wood cane. The Great Seer of All Seers is ready to meet his fans and greet the world!

A gnarled acacia wood cane rests at the entrance to Punxsutawney Phil's burrow door. The cane is used by the President of The Groundhog Club to knock on the door prior to Phil's public appearance.

The Groundhog Handler lifts Punxsutawney Phil high in the air amid the cheers of fans. Phil speaks to the President of the Groundhog Club first. "Scokakaplee," he says..."Good Morning to All!"

A proclamation is read aloud announcing the official forecast. Phil's forecast is broadcast around the world and recorded in the Congressional Record.

Members of the Inner Circle hold signs of Phil's forecast for the spectators to see.

Mr. James Means speaks to the crowd at Gobbler's Knob on Feb. 2. Mr. Means tells the audience, "Scokakaplee, Good Morning to All. True Believers here on Gobbler's Knob and around the world have just seen history in the making. He stood proud for a moment, then he saw his shadow at precisely 7:29 a.m."

Punxsutawney Phil poses for last minute publicity photographs and receives gifts from visiting guests. Then he dramatically retreats to his burrow to be with his wife, Philomena, and his cousin, Barney. Inside their warm burrow they will celebrate Groundhog Day with a special feast.

Another Groundhog Day has made history, thanks to the forecast of The Fearless Forecaster, Punxsutawney Phil!

Punxsutawney Phil also appears in his groundhog burrow in the Civic Center Zoo in Punxsutawney, Pa.

ABOUT THE AUTHOR AND ILLUSTRATOR:

Dr. Julia Spencer Moutran, a graduate of the University of Virginia and the University of Connecticut, is the author of **ELEMENTARY SCIENCE ACTIVITIES FOR ALL SEASONS, COLLECTING BUGS AND THINGS, ON LOCATION WITH BARBIE, THE SCIENCE TEACHER'S ALMANAC,** and six books on insects called **BUG PALS: LUCKY LADYBUG, FLASHING FIREFLY, MIGHTY MONARCH, BUSY BEE, CHIRPY CRICKET,** and **BUDDY BEETLE.** She is also the author of the **FIFTH GRADE TEACHER'S MONTH BY MONTH ACTIVITIES PROGRAM** to be published by Prentice-Hall.

Dr. Moutran has taught children from preschool through eighth grade. She lives in Avon, Connecticut with her husband, Alan, and their daughters, Meredith and Melanie. Meredith was born on Groundhog Day—February 2, 1982.

Mrs. Marsha (Dubnansky) Sweetland lived in Pennsylvania for nineteen years and taught art in the DuBois School System three of those years. She received her B.S. and M.Ed. Degrees in Art Education from the Pennsylvania State University.

Mrs. Sweetland is now a coordinator and teacher of art at William H. Hall High School in West Hartford, Connecticut, and she is co-owner of Willow Tree Gallery in Cromwell, Connecticut. She lives in West Hartford with her son, Kevin.

ORDER FORM

THE STORY OF PUNXSUTAWNEY PHIL, "THE FEARLESS FORECASTER"
by Julia Spencer Moutran, Ph.D.; Illustrated by Marsha Lewis Dubnansky.
WILL SPRING EVER COME TO GOBBLER'S KNOB?
by Julia Spencer Moutran, Ph.D.; Illustrated by Marsha Lewis Dubnansky.
64 page books available in paperback, hardback, and audiocassette with
full music, narration, and sound effects featuring Groundhog whistle and warble.
****

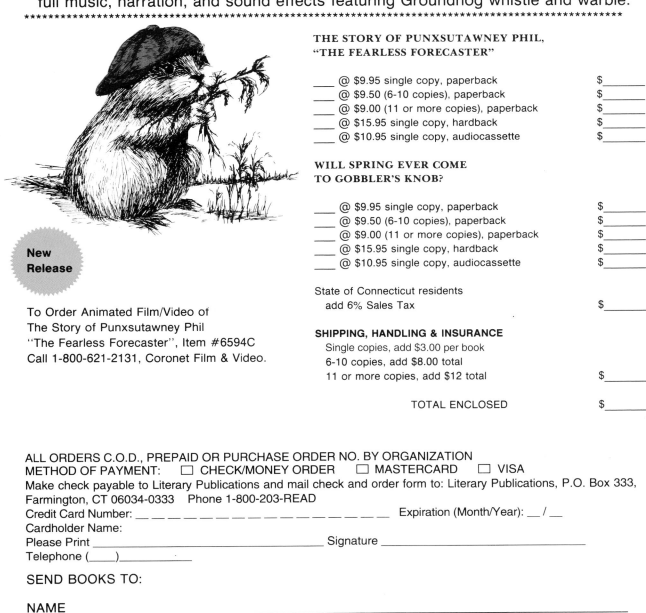

New Release

**THE STORY OF PUNXSUTAWNEY PHIL,
"THE FEARLESS FORECASTER"**

____ @ $9.95 single copy, paperback $_____
____ @ $9.50 (6-10 copies), paperback $_____
____ @ $9.00 (11 or more copies), paperback $_____
____ @ $15.95 single copy, hardback $_____
____ @ $10.95 single copy, audiocassette $_____

**WILL SPRING EVER COME
TO GOBBLER'S KNOB?**

____ @ $9.95 single copy, paperback $_____
____ @ $9.50 (6-10 copies), paperback $_____
____ @ $9.00 (11 or more copies), paperback $_____
____ @ $15.95 single copy, hardback $_____
____ @ $10.95 single copy, audiocassette $_____

State of Connecticut residents
  add 6% Sales Tax $_____

SHIPPING, HANDLING & INSURANCE
  Single copies, add $3.00 per book
  6-10 copies, add $8.00 total
  11 or more copies, add $12 total $_____

TOTAL ENCLOSED $_____

To Order Animated Film/Video of
The Story of Punxsutawney Phil
"The Fearless Forecaster", Item #6594C
Call 1-800-621-2131, Coronet Film & Video.

ALL ORDERS C.O.D., PREPAID OR PURCHASE ORDER NO. BY ORGANIZATION
METHOD OF PAYMENT: ☐ CHECK/MONEY ORDER ☐ MASTERCARD ☐ VISA
Make check payable to Literary Publications and mail check and order form to: Literary Publications, P.O. Box 333,
Farmington, CT 06034-0333   Phone 1-800-203-READ
Credit Card Number: __ __ __ __ __ __ __ __ __ __ __ __ __ __ __ __   Expiration (Month/Year): __ / __
Cardholder Name:
Please Print _____   Signature _____
Telephone (____)_____

SEND BOOKS TO:

NAME _____

STREET _____

CITY _____ STATE _____ ZIP _____